The Brothers and the Star Fruit Tree

A TALE FROM VIETNAM

Retold by Suzanne I. Barchers
Illustrated by Jamie Meckel Tablason

RED
CHAIR
·PRESS·

Please visit our website at **www.redchairpress.com**.
Find a free catalog of all our high-quality products for young readers.

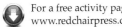 For a free activity page for this story, go to
www.redchairpress.com and look for Free Activities.

The Brothers and the Star Fruit Tree

Publisher's Cataloging-In-Publication Data
(Prepared by The Donohue Group, Inc.)

Barchers, Suzanne I.
   The brothers and the star fruit tree : a tale from Vietnam / retold by Suzanne I.
Barchers ; illustrated by Jamie Meckel Tablason.

   pages : illustrations ; cm. -- (Tales of honor)

   Summary: Two brothers' lives take different paths with one living a prosperous life
and one struggling to survive. But fate has a way of turning the tables in this popular
tale from Vietnam.
   Interest age level: 006-009.
   Issued also as an ebook.
   ISBN: 978-1-939656-83-4 (library binding)
   ISBN: 978-1-939656-84-1 (paperback)

   1. Brothers--Juvenile fiction. 2. Fruit trees--Juvenile fiction. 3. Wealth--Juvenile
fiction. 4. Folklore--Vietnam. 5. Brothers--Fiction. 6. Fruit trees--Fiction. 7. Wealth-
-Fiction. 8. Folklore--Vietnam. I. Thai, My Phuong. II. Title. III. Series: Barchers,
Suzanne. Tales of honor.

PZ8.1.B37 Sh 2015
398.2/73/09597   2014944305

This series first published by:
Red Chair Press LLC   PO Box 333   South Egremont, MA 01258-0333

Printed in the United States of America

WZ1114   1 2 3 4 5 18 17 16 15 14

Once upon a time, two brothers lived with their parents in a village in Vietnam. Over the years, the father worked hard and grew quite wealthy. He acquired much land and a fine house.

3

The brothers grew up in the same house with the same parents. Yet they were very different. One brother was content with a quiet, modest life.

The elder brother always wanted more—more wealth, more lands, and a bigger house.

In time, the parents grew frail and died. The elder son, now married, chose how the estate would be divided. Being a greedy man, he claimed most of the **inheritance**. He took the house, most of the land, and all of the money.

He sent the younger brother to live in a small house on a small piece of land. Some brothers might have complained about how unfair this was. But the younger brother was content with his good wife and his simple life.

One lonely tree grew on the younger brother's land. This star fruit tree would be a disappointment to most people. Its golden fruit was small and sour tasting.

But the younger brother saw its promise. He watered the tree every day. He trimmed its dead branches in hopes that they would grow. He longed to have it produce large amounts of fruit. Then he could sell the fruit and make a comfortable living.

Meanwhile, the elder brother enjoyed his wealth. He didn't worry about a thing—except how to spend his money.

The star fruit tree **flourished** under the younger brother's care. It grew tall and strong. When summer came, its branches drooped with the weight of the fruit. Once the star fruit was ripe, the younger brother prepared to harvest it.

But something stopped him. Each day, a very large raven alighted in the tree. It would eat its fill, moving from fruit to fruit. With each bite, the raven destroyed that piece of fruit. The raven was also destroying the man's hopes of earning a living.

The younger brother and his wife were **disheartened**. One day, they stood by the tree watching the raven eat.

"What are we going to do, Husband?" asked the young man's wife. "Every day the raven returns and eats the ripe fruit. If this continues, we may go hungry this winter."

"I know, my dear. But the raven must be hungry to come back every day. Once winter comes there will be no food for the raven to eat. At least we may be able to find other sources of food," he observed.

The raven, hearing the couple talk, perched on a low branch and spoke to them.

"Don't worry about using this fruit to make a living. I will reward you for sharing it with me," said the raven.

The couple stepped back in fear. Finding his voice at last, the man said, "We are happy to share with you. But we had hoped to have some fruit to sell. Otherwise, it will be a bitter winter for us."

"Trust me," said the raven. "I will repay you for the fruit and for your trust. Here is what to do. Go home and make a sack that is exactly three feet long. Bring the sack to the tree tomorrow. You will be well rewarded.

The next day, the younger brother took the sack to the tree. The raven was waiting in the tree, just as he had promised.

The raven flew down and said, "Climb on my back. Don't worry, I'm very strong. Bring the bag and hold on tightly."

The man's curiosity overcame his fear. He climbed on the raven's back, and they flew off to the sea.

After some time, the raven flew down and landed on an island. Gold and precious jewels lay all about, sparkling in the sun.

"Fill up the sack," the raven told him. "You and your wife will have enough to keep you in comfort for the rest of your lives."

"But won't the sack make me heavy? How will we return home?" the younger brother asked in concern.

"Your sack is exactly the right size, three feet long. I can fly us back, even when it's full," answered the raven.

Once they had safely returned, the man thanked the raven for his kindness.

He and his wife bought a larger piece of land and built a lovely new home. They lived comfortably, but did not spend in **excess**. They shared whatever they could with the poor.

One day, the couple invited the older brother and his wife to dinner. At first the older brother refused to come. But then he heard how the couple was living well, even sharing with the poor. The greedy brother just had to find out how this had happened.

So one night, the greedy brother and his wife came to dinner.

"Your home is fine, Brother." he said. "Tell me how you have managed to do so well?"

The younger brother shared the story about the raven and the star fruit tree. Of course, the greedy brother was **frantic** to own the tree and meet the raven.

"Trade with me!" he begged. "I'll give you all of my fortune if you let me have that star fruit tree!"

The younger brother agreed, and the exchange was made. The greedy brother waited by the star fruit tree each day.

As before, the raven came to eat its fill. The brother spoke to the raven, and it told him to bring back a three-foot long bag. In his greed, however, the brother brought a much bigger bag the next day.

The raven took the brother to the island and told him to fill up his bag. The greedy brother got to work. He filled up the bag. And when it was full, he filled up his pockets, and even his hat!

The greedy brother climbed onto the raven's back. It took off into the air, struggling with the weight of the gold and jewels. The raven flew back over the sea, straining with the extra weight of the larger bag. But even the strong raven couldn't keep going after some time.

The raven swayed and dipped. The greedy brother—and all his riches—slipped into the sea and was never seen again.

Each summer, the raven returns to the star fruit tree. And each summer, it eats its fill of the rich, ripe golden fruit. And the local people are happy to share their fruits with the hungry raven.

disheartened: to lose confidence or determination

excess: an amount of something that is more than needed

flourished: grew and developed successfully

frantic: wild with emotion

inheritance: money or property received on the death of someone

WHAT DO YOU THINK?

Question 1: Do you think the younger brother was wise to trust the raven?

Question 2: Why did the older brother trade his fortune for the star fruit tree?

Question 3: In what ways was the older brother shown to be greedy?

About Vietnamese Myths

The modern nation of Vietnam has a rich and long history of mythology. Even today, many people will say the origin of the Vietnamese people began with a dragon and a fairy princess. Myths and fables were often handed down through generations but most were not recorded or written down until the 13th century. Tales were used to help preserve the Vietnamese culture.

About the Author

After fifteen years as a teacher, Suzanne Barchers began a career in writing and publishing. She has written over 100 children's books, two college textbooks, and more than 20 reader's theater and teacher resource books. She previously held editorial roles at Weekly Reader and LeapFrog and is on the PBS Kids Media Advisory Board. Suzanne also plays the flute professionally – and for fun – from her home in Stanford, CA.

About the Illustrator

Jamie Tablason loves illustrating for children and the young at heart. Jamie received her BFA and MFA in Illustration from California State University. Sea creatures, California history, asian culture, and good food are a few things that inspire Jamie's work. She currently works and lives in Lakewood, California with her husband, and their two dogs, a basset hound and bulldog.